and the
School Play

Written by Tony Bradman

Illustrations by Susan Hellard

For Gabriel, son of
a great editor
T.B.

To Yvonne Chambers,
staff and children of
Oak Thorpe School
S.H.

First published in Great Britain 2002
by Egmont Books Ltd.
239 Kensington High Street, London W8 6SA
Text copyright © Tony Bradman 2002
Illustrations copyright © Susan Hellard 2002
The author and illustrator have asserted their moral rights.
Paperback ISBN 0 7497 4857 5
10 9 8 7 6 5 4 3 2 1
A CIP catalogue record for this title is available from the British Library.
Printed in Dubai

Contents

Red Bananas

Star of the Show

When Dilly came out of school one day a few weeks ago, it was easy to see he was excited about something. Mother was waiting for him in the crowd by the school gate, with Dilly's big sister Dorla. Dilly ran over to them.

'Guess what, Mother!' Dilly yelled, jumping up and down. 'My new teacher Miss Daffy says our class is going to put on a play!'

'That's nice, Dilly,' said Mother. 'What's the play called? And could you stop bouncing around like that? It's very annoying.'

'Sorry, Mother,' said Dilly, and stood still. 'It's called Dinorella! We'll be performing it for the whole school and parents can come too.'

'Really?' said Mother. 'Miss Daffy must be very brave.'

She'll be sorry.

'No she isn't,' said Dorla. 'She must be crazy! But then she wasn't here when Dilly and his class ruined the Christmas play last year.'

'Hey, it wasn't my fault!' said Dilly. 'Well, okay, some of it was. But I only started climbing on the scenery because I got bored waiting to say my one line. And I didn't start the argument between the girls and the boys, Dixie and Darryl did. Anyway, it will all be different this time!'

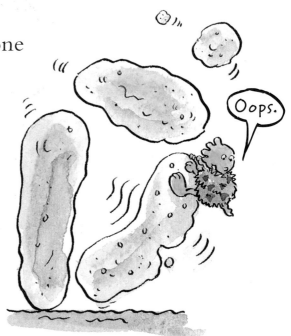

Oops.

7

'I hope you're right, Dilly,' said Mother.
Then a worried look passed across her face.
'Has Miss Daffy decided who gets which part?'

'Not yet,' said Dilly, running round in circles.
'She said she's still making up her mind, and
she'll tell us in the morning. But I'm bound to
get the main part, of course. I'm going to
be . . . THE STAR OF THE SHOW!'

'Er, hello?' said Dorla. 'Earth calling Dilly. I thought Dinorella was the main part in that story. Well, she's a girl! You're a boy, Dilly, remember?'

Dilly skidded to a halt, stared at Dorla, then opened his mouth wide, the way he does when he's about to let rip with an ultra-special, 150-mile-per-hour super-scream.

But he didn't. He suddenly snapped his
mouth shut and stood in a dramatic pose,
one paw against his forehead, eyes closed.

'That's it,'
Dilly moaned.
'My life is
over!'

'It's not
that bad,
Dilly,' said
Mother. She
seemed rather
surprised
Dilly hadn't
screamed. 'I'm
sure Miss
Daffy will
find you
another part.'

'Do you think so, Mother?' Dilly said in a quiet voice. He opened his eyes and looked up at her, paws clasped now, almost as if he were praying.

I can only hope.

'Oh yes, unless she *is* crazy,' Mother muttered under her breath. 'I think we've got a copy of Dinorella somewhere at home, Dilly,' she said. 'If you want, we can read it tonight to see what other parts there are in the story.'

'Great idea!' yelled Dilly, and scampered off along the street.

'Somehow I have a bad feeling about this,' said Mother.

The Prince or Nothing

That evening, Dilly made Mother and Father read him Dinorella over and over again.

Then he insisted they listen while he read it aloud to *them* over and over again. And you can guess what story he asked for at bedtime.

'So, Dinorella and The Prince lived happily ever after,' Father read out, and quickly closed the book. 'There you are, Dilly,' he said. 'I should think there's a part in that story for every little dinosaur in your class.'

'But I don't care about anybody else,' said Dilly with a frown. 'The only part that matters is the one I get. And I know which one I want.'

'Now now, Dilly,' said Father, 'that's not the right way to look at this. A play is a group effort, and it won't work unless you all pull together.'

'And you shouldn't pin your hopes on one particular part, Dilly,' said Mother. 'That means you'll only be disappointed if you don't get it.'

'But I am going to get it, Mother,' said Dilly, scowling. 'If I can't be Dinorella, then I'll have to be The Prince, of course!'

Mother sighed and glanced at Father, who rolled his eyes.

'Well,' said Mother, giving Dilly a strained smile, 'be a good little dinosaur and have a think about some of the other parts. Just in case, okay?'

'Okay, Mother,' said Dilly, sighing himself. 'If it makes you happy.'

Mother went through the other parts for boys in the story.

You could pull the pumpkin.

I don't think so.

There were several: Buttons, The Courtier
Who Carries The Lost Shoe, The Mice Who
Get Turned Into Horses To Pull The Magic
Coach.

'So, what do you think, Dilly?' said Father. 'Do you fancy any of those?'

'Umm,' murmured Dilly, striking a thoughtful pose. Then he grinned.

'No, I don't,' he said. 'It's The Prince, or nothing. Now, if you'll excuse me, I have to start getting ready for the most important day of my life.'

'Hang on, Dilly,' said Mother. 'I think you're making too much of this.'

'How can you possibly say that, Mother?' Dilly asked, his eyes gleaming. 'This could be the beginning of a whole new career for me. Today it might just be a school play, but soon it could be Hollywood!'

'Hey, does that mean you'll be leaving home?' Dorla asked as she went past Dilly's bedroom doorway. Dilly stuck his tongue out at her. Mother and Father just looked at each other with worried expressions.

Last but not Least

Dilly simply couldn't wait to get to school the next morning. Miss Daffy had promised to tell the class after assembly who would be playing each part.

'Settle down, class,' said Miss Daffy. 'Now, before I start, I want you to know I think you're *all* brilliant. Making my mind up has been very hard.'

'Please, Miss!' said Dilly impatiently. 'Could you just get on with it?'

'Oh, right,' said Miss Daffy. 'The part of Dinorella goes to . . . Dixie.'

Dixie squealed, and the other girls hugged her and squealed too.

'Huh,' said Dilly. 'I suppose she'll be okay. Not great, just okay.'

'What do you mean?' said Dixie. 'I'm going to be absolutely fabulous!'

'Hey, Dilly, you leave our Dixie alone,' said Doris, Dixie's friend.

'She'll make a terrific Dinorella,' said Davina, Dixie's other friend.

'And you two will make a great pair of ugly sisters,' muttered Dilly. 'What about the main boy's part, then, Miss? I mean The Prince?'

23

'Er . . . all in good time, Dilly,' said Miss
Daffy, nervously. She carried on, announcing
who was going to play Dinorella's Father,
Buttons, The Wicked Stepmother and the
other speaking parts. Finally there was only
one part left to announce. 'And last but not
least,' said Miss Daffy, 'the
part of The Prince
goes to . . . ' Dilly stood
up and smiled. 'Darryl!'
said Miss Daffy.

Yippee!

'Wow, thanks Miss!' said Darryl. 'I promise I won't let you down.'

'But . . .' said Dilly. 'That's the part I want, Miss! I'd be fantastic! I've worked it out already. I'd have a big sword and climb on the scenery and jump off and fight everybody . . .' Dilly looked at Miss Daffy and realised he'd said the wrong thing. 'I definitely won't get the part now, will I?' he said.

ut, Miss . . .
m the star!

That'll teach him!

'No, Dilly,' said Miss Daffy in a gentle
voice. 'I'm sorry, but I don't think
you will. I'm sure I can find you a non-
speaking role, though.'

'That serves you right, Dilly,' Darryl
sneered. 'I'm really going to enjoy being The
Prince!'

'I wouldn't be so smug if I were you,
Darryl,' laughed Dudley, who would be
playing Buttons. 'You have to kiss Dixie at
the end of the play.'

'Ugh, yuck and double yuck!' yelled Darryl. 'Not me!'

'I'm not kissing you either, ugly mug!' yelled Dixie.

'You tell him, Dixie!' yelled Davina and Doris.

Suddenly the whole class was arguing and shouting.

'That will do, class!' said Miss Daffy. 'Quiet, please!'

But Dilly was quiet already. Quiet, and very miserable.

Disappointed Dilly

At supper that night, Dilly wasn't his usual
lively self. He sat at the table with a long
face, hardly said a word, and didn't do
anything naughty at all. Mother and Father
were even more worried now, and tried to
cheer him up.

'Come on, Dilly, eat your food,' said
Father, smiling. 'It's your favourite, marsh-
worm spaghetti with sticky mud sauce. I
cooked it especially for you.'

'Thanks, Father,' Dilly murmured. 'But I'm just not hungry.'

'There's fern-flake ice-cream for dessert, Dilly,' said Mother.

'Is there?' Dilly sighed. 'I don't want any of that, either.'

'Hey, terrific!' said Dorla, happily. 'All the more for me!'

You can have bugs on top.

As a special treat.

'That will do, Dorla,' Father said. 'You're not being very helpful.'

'No, you're not,' said Mother. 'Can't you see your brother is upset?'

'Ooooh, sorry I spoke,' said Dorla. She folded her arms and sulked.

'Do you want to talk, Dilly?' said Mother. 'Have you had a bad day?'

'You did get a part in the play, didn't you?' Father asked, anxiously.

'Well, yes,' Dilly murmured. 'And no.'

'I don't understand,' said Mother. 'Either you got a part or you didn't.'

'I did,' said Dilly. 'But I don't have any words to say.'

'Ah, I see,' said Father. 'Well, what part did you get, exactly?'

Dilly lowered his head and spoke so quietly none of them could hear.

'What did you say, Dilly?' Mother asked. 'You'll have to speak up.'

'I'M AN EXTRA!' yelled Dilly. 'One of
The Dinosaurs At The Ball!'

'So you're not going to be *the star of the show* then?' said Dorla.

'Dorla!' Mother and Father yelled, both of them expecting Dilly to fire off an ultra-special, 150-mile-per-hour super-scream now. But he didn't.

Uh oh!

Here goes.

'I'm an extra!'

'No, I'm not,' Dilly said, his bottom lip quivering, his eyes damp. 'Miss Daffy obviously doesn't realise that I'm a young dinosaur of great talent.'

'No, I'm quite sure she doesn't,' said Mother. 'Although perhaps ...'

'But I'm no dummy!'

'But if she expects me to stand there like some kind of stuffed dummy,' growled Dilly fiercely, 'well then, she might be in for a BIG surprise!'

'I hope you're not planning to be naughty, Dilly,' said Father.

'Can I leave the table?' said Dilly. Mother and Father glanced at each other, then nodded at him. Dilly swept out of the room, his snout in the air.

'I think we'd better have a word with Miss Daffy,' said Father.

'I couldn't agree more, dear,' said Mother. Dorla just scowled.

The Big Day

The next day, Mother and Father did go into school to speak to Miss Daffy. And when Dilly came out of school later, he was looking much happier.

'I'm so glad you told me how Dilly felt, Mr and Mrs Dinosaur,' Miss Daffy whispered to them at the school gate. 'I hope he'll be okay now.'

'Oh, I'm sure he will be,' said Father. 'It was a brilliant idea of yours to have a narrator for the play, and to give Dilly the part!'

'Yes, so he gets to say a lot,' said Mother, 'but he has to stay in one place and isn't allowed to run around causing chaos. I'm impressed, Miss Daffy.'

'Huh, I'm not,' Dorla muttered. 'I'll bet he still manages to misbehave.'

I hope I can trust him.

'Oh, I do hope not,' said Miss Daffy. 'It would be so embarrassing!'

'Come on, Mother and Father!' said Dilly. 'Can we go home now?'

Over the next few days, Dilly made
Mother and Father listen to him while
he practised his words over and over again.

Eventually The Big Day came. The school
hall was filling up rapidly when Mother and
Father arrived and took their seats, right at
the front. Dorla was allowed to sit with them.

'It's rather noisy in here, don't you think?'
said Mother.

It *was* noisy in the hall. Every class in the school was there, and lots of adults. All the young dinosaurs were chattering with excitement, the grown-ups were calling out loudly to each other, and several babies were crying.

'And Miss Daffy's class seem to be arguing!' said Father.

It was true. The little dinosaurs in Miss Daffy's class were in their costumes, and they were supposed to be waiting quietly at the side of the stage. But there was a lot of pushing and shoving and hissing going on.

'Stop that immediately, class!' Miss Daffy said, crossly.

'The boys started it, Miss!' said Dixie. 'They're nasty!'

It was her, Miss!

'Don't listen to her, Miss,' said Darryl. 'It was the girls!'

'Well, I don't care who started it,' said Miss Daffy, 'I'm stopping it. Let's get on with the play, shall we? Dilly, you'd better do the introduction, okay?'

Dilly stepped forward eagerly. 'Welcome to our play everybody,' he said. But the audience was making too much noise, and Dilly's classmates were arguing, so nobody heard. 'WELCOME TO OUR PLAY, EVERYBODY!' said Dilly, raising his voice. But still nobody heard him or took any notice.

Ahem.

'This is going to be such a disaster!' Miss Daffy wailed. Mother and Father were looking at Dilly anxiously, wondering what he was going to do.

Stand back, Miss Daffy.

'Oh no it won't be, Miss,' said Dilly, grimly. 'They're not spoiling this,' he muttered to himself, 'not after all it's taken me to get this part, anyway.'

Then he struck a dramatic pose, opened his mouth, and fired off an ultra-special, 150-mile-per-hour super-scream. Everybody — the whole audience, and all of Dilly's classmates — was so stunned they fell into total silence.

Mother and Father were horrified. Then they realised what Dilly had done, and started to grin. In a strange way it was something of a relief to hear Dilly doing his scream again. Even Dorla couldn't help smiling.

'Now, as I was trying to say,' continued Dilly. 'Welcome to our play.'

'Thanks, Dilly,' Miss Daffy whispered to him. 'I don't know what I would have done without you. You really are the star of the show!'

But then we always knew he would be, didn't we?

That's me!